瓦莱丽·托马斯

出生于澳大利亚墨尔本的瓦莱丽，一定是特别热爱魔法世界，才能把女巫温妮的故事写得这么妙趣横生、引人入胜。当然，这也跟瓦莱丽喜欢孩子、熟知孩子的内心有关。她在澳大利亚和英国当过老师，写出过许多让孩子们爱不释手的故事。瓦莱丽还喜欢到世界各地旅行，把旅行中的五彩心情都变成了斑斓有趣的书。她一定想过："要是我有一把飞天扫帚就好啦，想去哪儿就去哪儿！"

科奇·保罗

画出了女巫温妮的科奇·保罗有一个让人羡慕的童年——整天在非洲的韦尔德草原上无拘无束地玩耍，难怪他有这么丰富的想象力！更何况，科奇·保罗还刻苦地学习了美术和影视动画，努力让自己成为"世界上最伟大的肖像画家"。为了画出孩子们最喜欢的作品，科奇·保罗经常去学校，在和孩子们的交往中激发创作灵感。科奇·保罗和两个孩子住在英国的牛津，不过每到夏天，他们都会去希腊享受一下爱琴海上灿烂无比的阳光。

任溶溶

一个精通俄文、英文、意大利文、日文等多种文字的翻译家，一个写出过很多儿童诗歌、童话、儿童小说的好玩儿的作家，一个得过国际儿童读物联盟翻译奖、亚洲儿童文学奖、陈伯吹儿童文学奖杰出贡献奖、宋庆龄儿童文学奖特殊贡献奖等一连串奖的可爱的老先生。他总是生活得特别带劲儿，像挥动魔法棒的女巫温妮那样，兴致勃勃地去经历生活中的每一件事。

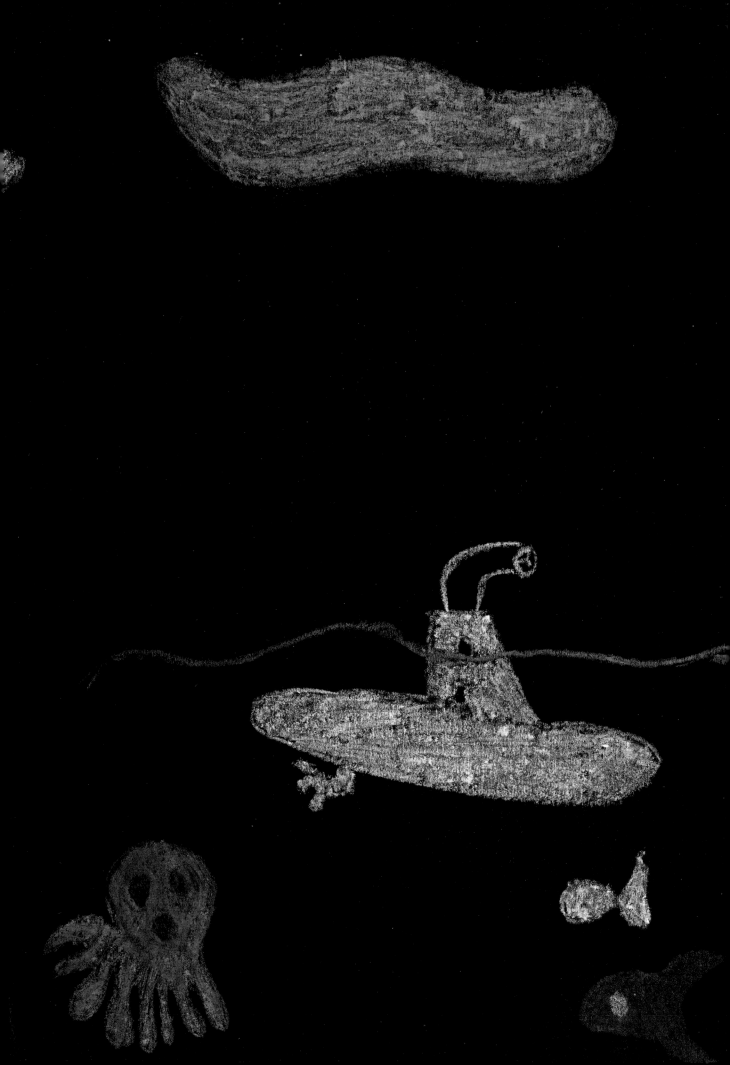

京权图字：01-2012-5383

图书在版编目(CIP)数据

温妮去潜水/（澳）托马斯（Thomas, V.）著；（英）保罗（Paul, K.）绘；任溶溶译.— 北京：外语教学与研究出版社，2012.11
（温妮女巫魔法绘本）
书名原文：Winnie under the Sea
ISBN 978-7-5135-2555-8

Ⅰ．①温…　Ⅱ．①托…②保…③任…　Ⅲ．①儿童文学—图画故事—澳大利亚—现代
Ⅳ．①I611.85

中国版本图书馆 CIP 数据核字 (2012) 第 264477 号

悠游网—外语学习 一网打尽
www.2u4u.com.cn
阅读、视听、测试、交流、共享
提供海量电子文档、视频、MP3、手机应用下载！

出　版　人：蔡剑峰
策划编辑：吉劲秋　周　英
责任编辑：刘秀玲
装帧设计：许　岚
出版发行：外语教学与研究出版社
社　　址：北京市西三环北路 19 号（100089）
网　　址：http://www.fltrp.com
印　　刷：北京十月印刷有限公司
开　　本：889×1194　1/16
印　　张：2.5
版　　次：2012 年 11 月第 1 版　2012 年 11 月第 1 次印刷
书　　号：ISBN 978-7-5135-2555-8
定　　价：14.90 元
＊　　＊　　＊
购书咨询：(010)88819929　电子邮箱：club@fltrp.com
如有印刷、装订质量问题，请与出版社联系
联系电话：(010)61207896　电子邮箱：zhijian@fltrp.com
制售盗版必究　举报查实奖励
版权保护办公室举报电话：(010)88817519
物料号：225550001

温妮女巫
魔法绘本

Winnie under the Sea
温妮去潜水

（澳）瓦莱丽·托马斯/文 （英）科奇·保罗/图

任溶溶/译

外语教学与研究出版社
FOREIGN LANGUAGE TEACHING AND RESEARCH PRESS
北京 BEIJING

女巫温妮和她的大黑猫威尔伯打算去度假。

"威尔伯，今年我们去哪儿呢？"温妮问道。
她在网上查到了一个小岛，
那里有蔚蓝的大海、金色的沙滩和成片的椰树林。

2

各种漂亮的鱼在蔚蓝色的海水里游来游去。
"威尔伯，这些鱼看起来很可爱吧？"温妮说。
"它们看起来很好吃。"威尔伯心想。
"我们就去那儿吧！"温妮说。

3

温妮收拾好行李箱，
威尔伯跳上她的肩膀，
他们一下子就冲上了天空。

温妮和威尔伯终于看到了小岛，
它看上去确实很迷人。

他们降落在金色的沙滩上，
然后找到了一间舒适的小屋。

5

温妮穿上脚蹼，戴上泳镜，一头扎进了水里。

威尔伯则爬到了一棵椰子树上面。
太好玩儿了！
过了一会儿，他趴在树上睡着了。
真安逸呀！

温妮玩得很开心。
海里到处都是鱼，
还有海豚、海龟和珊瑚。
真是太美了！
温妮想让威尔伯也来看一看。

"威尔伯！"温妮喊道，
"快来看看这些鱼，
你一定会喜欢的！"

威尔伯也想看看那些鱼。
他把一只爪子伸进了水里。
唔！讨厌！爪子湿了！
"喵——呜！"威尔伯大叫一声。
他讨厌把身上弄得湿淋淋的。

这时，温妮想到了一个
绝妙的好主意。
她挥动魔法棒，
大喊一声——

阿布拉卡达布拉！

威尔伯不再是
一只猫了。

他变成了一条"猫鱼"！

"猫鱼"威尔伯纵身一跃，
跳入海中，
欢快地游了起来。

温妮透过泳镜看着威尔伯。

他一会儿追着小鱼到处跑，
一会儿又潜到一只狗鲨下面，
和一只小龙虾玩起了接球游戏。

看到"猫鱼"威尔伯玩得这么开心，
温妮也想变成一条鱼了。

但是她不能变成鱼，
变成鱼就没办法拿魔法棒了。
那变成什么好呢？
有了！

温妮挥动魔法棒，大喊一声——

阿布拉卡达布拉！

温妮变成了一只八爪鱼——
一只长着橙黄相间的腿，
还拿着魔法棒的
八爪鱼！

变成八爪鱼真好玩儿！
八爪鱼温妮舞动着八条腿，
穿过海藻，绕过珊瑚，爬过岩石。

"猫鱼"威尔伯在她身边钻来钻去，
成千上万条鱼与他们一同游戏，
有小鱼，有大鱼，有……
突然——

一只海狮出现了！

海狮尾巴轻轻一弹，温妮的魔法棒就掉了。

她急忙去抓魔法棒，但没抓着。

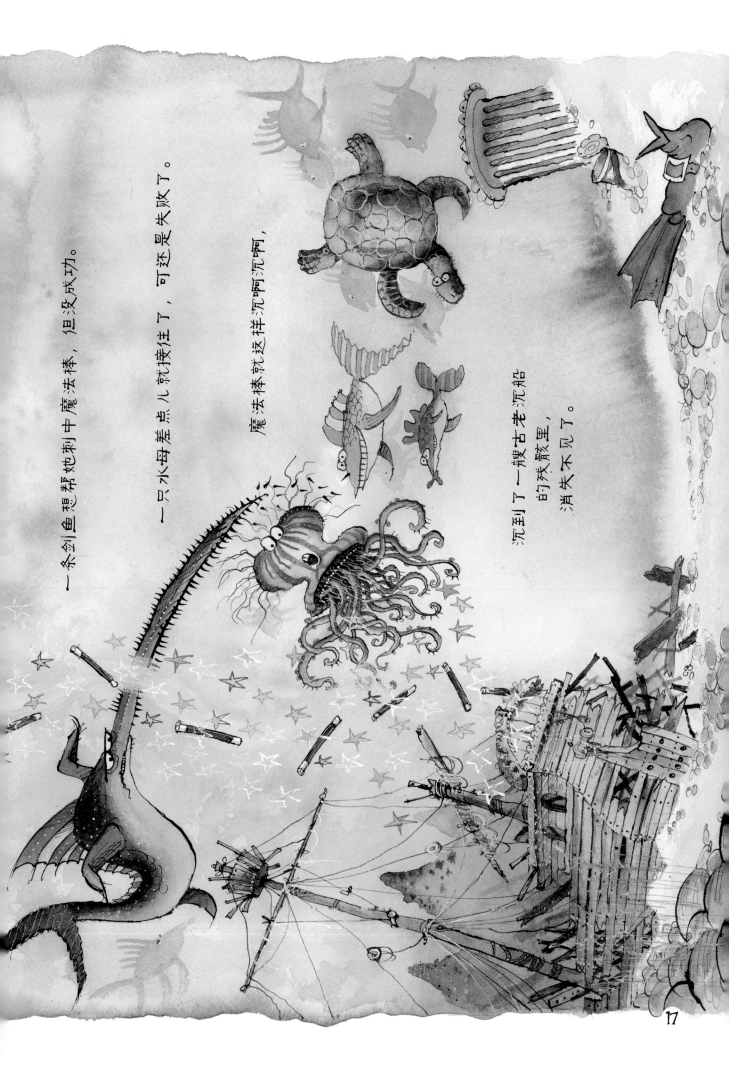

一条剑鱼想帮她刺中魔法棒，但没成功。

一只水母差点儿就接住了，可还是失败了。

魔法棒就这样沉啊沉啊，

沉到了一艘古老沉船
的残骸里，
消失不见了。

"真是糟糕透顶！"温妮大喊起来。
但她的声音在水里听起来就像是
"咕嘟，咕嘟，咕嘟"。
"咕嘟，咕嘟，咕嘟。"威尔伯也大喊起来。

他们可不想永远呆在海里。
魔法棒到底掉到哪儿去了呢？
卡在锚里了？没有。

在绳子下面？没有。　　　　　　　　在大螃蟹后面？没有。

威尔伯把魔法棒往上一扔，
温妮一把抓住魔法棒，
连挥五下，然后大喊一声——

阿布拉卡达布拉！

在藏宝箱里？没错！

女巫温妮和黑猫威尔伯又回到了海滩上。

"这可真刺激呀，威尔伯！"温妮说，
"但有点儿太刺激了。我们以后可不能再这么玩了。
不过，海底可真美啊！"

这时，温妮又想到了一个绝妙的好主意。

她看到海面上漂着一艘黄色的小船。
于是她挥动魔法棒，大喊一声——

GHOTI

阿布拉卡达布拉！

这时，海面上出现了……

一艘黄色的潜水艇。

温妮和威尔伯钻了进去。
鱼儿们都游到潜水艇的窗户外面，
好奇地往里面张望。

"海底真是美极了，你说是吗，威尔伯？"温妮说。
"这儿不仅美，还不会把身上弄湿。"威尔伯想。
"咕噜噜，咕噜噜，咕噜噜。"他满意地哼道。

Winnie under the Sea

It was holiday time for Winnie the Witch
and her big black cat, Wilbur.

"Where will we go this year, Wilbur?" asked Winnie.
She searched the internet and found a little island,
with blue sea, golden sand, and coconut trees.

The bright blue sea was full of beautiful fish.
"Don't the fish look lovely, Wilbur?" she said.
"They look delicious," thought Wilbur.
"That's where we'll go," said Winnie.

She packed her suitcase,
Wilbur jumped onto her shoulder,
and they zoomed up into the sky.

At last, there was the island.

It did look lovely.

They landed on the golden sand,
and found a comfortable hut.

Winnie put on her flippers and her goggles,
and dived into the water.

Wilbur climbed a coconut tree.
That was fun.
Then he had a sleep.
That was peaceful.

Winnie was having a lovely time.
The sea was full of fish.
There were dolphins, turtles, and coral.
It was so beautiful.

Winnie wanted Wilbur to see it, too.

"Wilbur," called Winnie,
"come and see the fish.
You'll love them!"

Wilbur wanted to see the fish.
He put one paw in the water.

Erk! Nasty! It was wet!
"Meeeeooow!" cried Wilbur.
He hated getting wet.

Then Winnie had a wonderful idea.
She waved her magic wand, shouted,
"ABRACADABRA!"

And Wilbur was no longer a cat.

He was a cat-fish!

Wilbur the cat-fish dived into
the waves and swam away.

Winnie watched him through her goggles.

He chased some tiny fish.
Then he dived under a dogfish
and played catch with a crayfish.

Wilbur the cat-fish was having so much fun,
Winnie wanted to be a fish as well.

But she couldn't be a fish.
She had to hold her magic wand.
What could she be?
Of course!

Winnie waved her wand, shouted
"ABRACADABRA!"

And she was an octopus!
An octopus with orange and yellow legs,
holding a magic wand!

It was fun being an octopus.
Winnie the octopus waved her eight legs
and floated through the seaweed,
around the coral, over the rocks.

Wilbur the cat-fish darted around her.
Thousands of fish swam with them.
Tiny fish, big fish, and, suddenly...

A sea lion.

The sea lion flipped its tail,

and Winnie lost her wand.

She grabbed at it, but missed.

A swordfish tried to spear it for her,
but missed.

A jellyfish nearly caught it, but missed.

Down, down it sank,
into the wreck of an old sailing ship,
and disappeared.

"Blithering broomsticks!" wailed Winnie,
but it sounded like, "Bubble, bubble, bubble."
"Bubble, bubble, bubble," cried Wilbur.

They didn't want to stay under the sea for ever.
Where was the magic wand?
Stuck in the anchor? No.

Under the ropes? No.

Behind the big crab? No.

In the treasure chest? Yes!

Wilbur flipped it out.
Winnie grabbed it,
waved it five times, shouted,
"ABRACADABRA!"

And a witch and a cat floated back to the shore.

"That was exciting, Wilbur," Winnie said.
"Too exciting. We won't do that again.
But it is beautiful under the sea."

Then Winnie had another wonderful idea.

A little yellow boat was bobbing on the waves.
Winnie waved her magic wand, shouted,
"ABRACADABRA!"

And there, bobbing on the waves...

Was a yellow submarine.

Winnie and Wilbur went on board.
The fish swam up to the windows and looked in.

"It is lovely under the sea, isn't it, Wilbur," said Winnie.
"It's lovely and dry in here," Wilbur thought.
"Purr, purr, purr," he said.